Chicken Fingers, Mac and Cheese...

WHY DO YOU ALWAYS HAVE TO SAY PLEASE?

By Wendy Rosen and Jackie End

Illustrated by Cheryl Tuck-Bernstein

MODERN
PUBLISHING
A DIVISION OF
UNISYSTEMS, INC.

New York, New York

Text and Art Copyright ©2005 Modern Publishing,
a division of Unisystems, Inc. All Rights Reserved.

Published by Modern Publishing, a division of Unisystems, Inc.
No part of this publication may be reproduced, stored in a retrieval system,
or transmitted in any form without written permission from the publisher.

Modern Publishing
A Division of Unisystems, Inc.
New York, New York
Printed in Italy
modernpublishing.com

2 4 6 8 10 9 7 5 3

Library of Congress Cataloging-in-Publication Data Pending

For
Neil Rosen   Mama Lil
Grace and Joe Arlotta

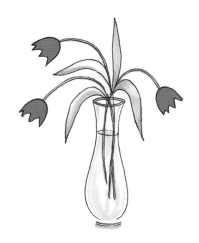

One of Lily's favorite things
is going out to eat.

She loves to go to restaurants.
For her it's such a treat.

Manners are important.
Lily knows it's true.
'Cause manners make things nicer
in everything you do.

It's best to say please for whatever you want.
It's best to say please in a restaurant.

Because it's just good manners, Max.

Lily has a restaurant voice.
It's never loud or whiney.

She knows how
to say "Thank You,"
and just where
to keep her hiney.

No whining when dining.
It just isn't fair,
to all of the people who like quiet air.

Sitting up on your knees is very unnerving,
and to other people, it's even disturbing.

Put your napkin on your lap,
not on your head.

Keep your elbows off the table...
and never, ever play dead.

One plate, two plate, three plate, four.
Does anybody know
what all this stuff is for?

dinner fork

salad fork

Salad fork This can be for salad or any other first course – except soup. Soup would run right through it.

Dinner fork This is for the main course.

napkin

Napkin This is for wiping schmootz from your mouth and hands.

teaspoon

Soup spoon This pretty much explains itself, don't you think?

knife

soup spoon

Teaspoon You know, for tea. Or maybe ice cream.

Knife This is for the main course unless you need to cut something in the first course – then it's for both.

Trying new things isn't always a treat.
Once Lily saw someone eating pigs' feet.

She wanted to yell, "Eww, that is so yucky!"
But she kept nice and quiet...
boy, were her parents lucky!

Max likes wontons and lots of fried rice.

Lily thinks pizza with olives is nice.

Especially when she shares it... with her friend, Ben Bryce.

But today their parents had a big surprise,
Lily and Max got chicken potpies!

Talking with your mouth full is totally rude.
No one wants to see all that chewed up food.

When you're eating soup,
try not to slurp.
When you're feeling full,
try not to burp.

These things
can happen,
they're really
no big deal.

Just say
"Excuse me" or "I'm sorry"
and go right back to your meal.

Some kids pile on the fries,
because they think they're yummy.

Sometimes their eyes
are much bigger than their tummies.

When someone's drinking milk,
please don't make them laugh.

Or out of their nose. . . a big white splash!

Never throw food. It's rude and it's messy.

And you'd feel just awful,
if you hit someone's Aunt Tessie.

It's much better to smile
and be polite.
To respect other people,
you know that's right.

Manners are important.
Now Max knows it's true.

'Cause manners make things nicer
in everything you do.

MANNERS

1. It's best to say "Please" and "Thank you."
2. No whining when dining.
3. Stay in your seat.
4. Keep your napkin on your lap.
5. Elbows off the table.
6. Don't talk with your mouth full.
7. Say "Excuse me" when you burp or slurp.
8. Don't let your eyes get bigger than your tummy.
9. When someone's drinking, don't make them laugh.
10. No throwing food.